Grobblechops is based on a tale from *Masnavi*,
one of the best-known and most influential
works by Rumi, a thirteenth century poet,
philosopher and Sufi mystic.

#Grobblechops

Copyright © Tiny Owl Publishing 2019
Text © Elizabeth Laird 2019
Illustrations © Jenny Lucander 2019

Elizabeth Laird has asserted her right under the Copyright, Designs
and Patents Act 1988 to be identified as Author of this work

Jenny Lucander as asserted her right under the Copyright, Designs
and Patents Act 1988 to be identified as Illustrator of this work

First published in the UK in 2019 by Tiny Owl Publishing, London

www.tinyowl.co.uk

A catalogue record for this book is available from the British Library.

ISBN 978-1-910328-41-5

Printed in China

GROBBLECHOPS

Elizabeth Laird Jenny Lucander

TINY OWL

Amir didn't want to go to bed.

"No!" he shouted. "I won't! No-o-o!"

"Why not?" said his dad. "Your bed's all cosy
and warm, and look, Teddy's waiting for you,
right there on the pillow."

"But I'm scared of the dark," said Amir. "There might be a-a-a..."

"A what?" said Dad.

"...a monster," whispered Amir.

"He might come in the night, and he might have **huge teeth** and growl like **a lion**. He might try to eat me."

"Well," said Dad. "If he does come, show him your teeth and growl even **louder.** Like **a tiger.** You can be really scary when you try, Amir.

You'll terrify him."

"But what if he's **not scared**? What if he **doesn't** run away but just stands there and then jumps on me and eats me up?"

"If he tries any of that nonsense," said Amir's dad, "you'll call for me and I'll come running in with my frying pan, and I'll shake it at him. That'll do the trick."

"But what if my monster's got a dad too?" said Amir.

"And what if he shouts for him, and he comes, and his frying pan's bigger than yours, and he eats you up while the little monster's eating me?"

"In that case," said his dad, "we'll call for your mum, and she'll come with her big umbrella and she'll flap it in the big monster's face, and he'll be so scared he'll go down on his knees and beg for mercy."`

"But suppose the monster's dad isn't scared **at all**, and suppose he fights my mum and tries to **eat her**, while the monster's mum is trying to **eat you**?"

"Oh, I don't think that would happen," said his dad.

"Grown-ups, even grown-up monsters, like arguing more than fighting. Fighting's too tiring, especially in the evenings. So while your mum and I are arguing with the grown-up monsters, you and the little monster can go off and play."

Amir thought about this.

"I don't know how to play with a monster," he said. "I don't know what sort of things he likes doing."

"You know what?" said his dad. "I think he'd like it if you showed him your toy cars. Poor little monster. I bet he hasn't got any of his own."

"And," said his dad, "when the grown-ups see how nicely you and your little monster are playing, we'll stop arguing and sit down for a cup of coffee to talk things over."

Amir picked up his teddy and held him tight as he climbed into bed. "I wouldn't let my monster touch Teddy," he said bravely.

"Of course not," said his dad. "But he won't want to. He'll be too busy having fun with your toy cars."

He kissed Amir goodnight and went out of the room, leaving the door open so that a bit of light could come in.

"Oh, I forgot," he said, putting his head back round the door. "Has your monster got a name?"

"Yes," said Amir sleepily.

"He's called Grobblechops, and he likes my pick-up truck best."

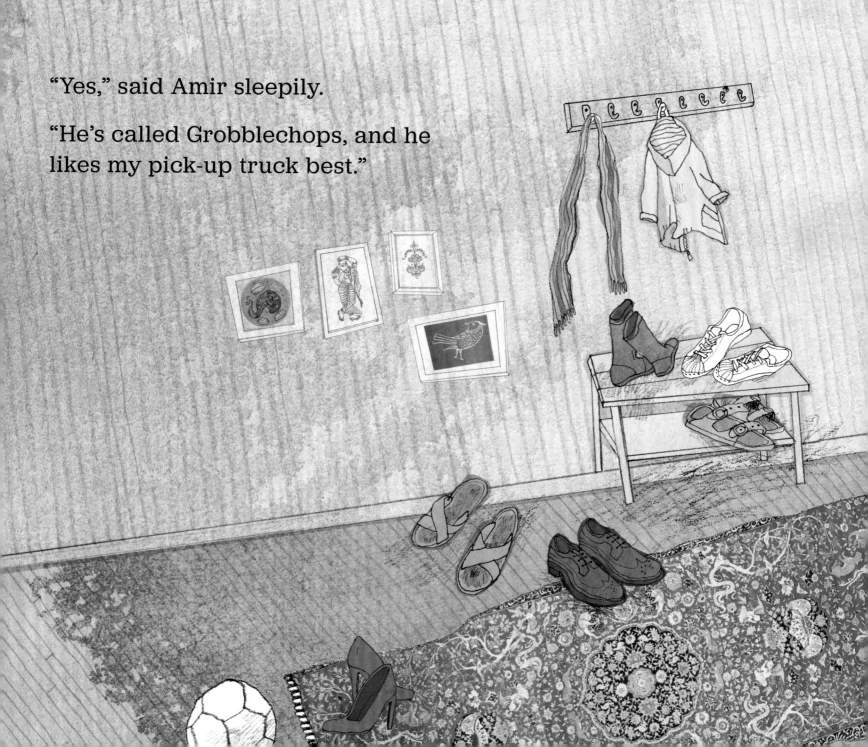